MR. NOSEY
and the Beanstalk

Roger Hargreaves

Original concept by
Roger Hargreaves

Written and illustrated by
Adam Hargreaves

Mr Nosey is one of those people who is curious about everything.

If he comes across a parcel he will start to wonder what's inside it.

And the more curious he becomes the more he has to know.

And even if it is addressed to someone else, Mr Nosey will not be able to stop himself opening it.

Just to have a look.

His curiosity always gets the better of him.

One day, Mr Nosey was out for a walk when he met a Wizard. The Wizard was holding a small bag.

Mr Nosey, being Mr Nosey, had to know what was inside the bag.

The Wizard told him that it was a bag full of magic beans.

Mr Nosey had to know what was magic about them.

"I will give you one bean," said the Wizard. "And if you take it home and plant it, you will find out. That is, if you're sure that you want to find out."

What a silly question. Of course Mr Nosey was sure he wanted to find out!

At home, Mr Nosey planted the bean in his garden. The next morning he could not believe his eyes.

There in the middle of his garden was a giant beanstalk that stretched up into the clouds.

As Mr Nosey admired the beanstalk a thought occured to him.

"What could be at the top of the beanstalk?"

The more he thought this thought, the more curious he became, and the more curious he became, the more he had to know.

So he began to climb the beanstalk.

He climbed . . .

. . . and he climbed . . .

. . . and he climbed. Right up into the clouds.
And when he reached the top he could not believe
his eyes. (For the second time that day.) There in the
clouds was a giant castle!

And then a thought occurred to him.

"Who might live in a castle in the clouds?"

And the thought grew into curiosity, and the curiosity
got the better of him. So he set out across the clouds
to the castle.

The giant castle had a giant door, and in the giant door there was a giant keyhole.

Mr Nosey cannot pass a keyhole and resist the urge to have a peek, and this time was no different.

Except that this time it was different because Mr Nosey could fit through the keyhole.

Once inside, it quickly became apparent that the 'who' who lived in the castle was a giant.

Now you or I would have sensibly left as fast as we could.

In fact, we would not have been there in the first place. But Mr Nosey, as you can guess, could not resist having a look around.

Mr Nosey went into the Giant's kitchen and in the corner were three small cupboards. Of course Mr Nosey had to know what was inside them.

He opened the first cupboard. Inside was a small bag.

Before he could look inside the bag he heard a terrifying sound.

THUMP!

THUMP!

THUMP!

It was the thud of the Giant's heavy-booted footsteps, somewhere in the castle, and they were getting closer.

Mr Nosey grabbed the bag, scrambled through the keyhole and slithered back down the beanstalk as fast as he could.

Safely back at home he discovered that the bag was full of gold coins!

That night he could not sleep. He lay in bed thinking about the other two cupboards.

"What could they contain?"

He just had to know.

Early the next morning back up the beanstalk went Mr Nosey, back through the keyhole and back to the second cupboard in the Giant's kitchen.

Inside it was a hen.

"That's curious," thought Mr Nosey to himself, not for the first time in this story!

He picked up the hen and there was a golden egg.

"A hen that lays golden eggs," murmured Mr Nosey. "I'll need to take this home for a closer look."

Just then Mr Nosey heard the heavy boots of the Giant coming down the stairs.

THUMP!

THUMP!

THUMP!

Mr Nosey tucked the hen under his arm and ran for his life.

The hen fascinated Mr Nosey, but it did not stop him thinking about the third cupboard. He was terrified of the Giant, but his curiosity overcame his fear and so, the following morning, back to the Giant's kitchen he went.

He opened the third cupboard and in it was a golden harp.

A golden harp that was singing!

Mr Nosey sat and listened to the harp. He felt safe, knowing that he would be able to hear the Giant's loud boots coming.

But the Giant was wearing his slippers that morning, which is how he caught Mr Nosey.

"So you're the thief!" boomed the Giant. "I have a mind to grind your bones to make my bread!"

Mr Nosey's eyes nearly popped out of his head.

"But I won't," continued the Giant. "I prefer cornflakes for breakfast. Now, I know what to do with you. Since you are so interested in what is in my cupboards, you can clean them out for me."

And Mr Nosey did.

It took him three whole days.

Giant's cupboards are . . . well, giant.

"Now let that be a lesson to you," said the Giant.

And you'd think it would have been, but the very next day Mr Nosey came upon an empty house and the front door was open and on the kitchen table were three bowls of porridge . . .

. . . but that's another story.